HIGH SCHOOL MUSICAL

Book of the Film
Adapted by N.B. Grace
Based on the Disney Channel Original Movie
"High School Musical", written by Peter Barsocchini

Pages 8-9, 112: "Start of Something New" by Matthew Gerard and Robbie Nevil ©
2005 Walt Disney Music Company (ASCAP); pages 30-31: "Get'cha Head in the
Game" by Ray Cham, Greg Cham, and Andrew Seeley © 2005 Walt Disney Music
Company (ASCAP) and Five Hundred South Songs (SESAC); page 64: "What I've
Been Looking For" by Andy Dodd and Adam Watts © 2005 Walt Disney Music
Company (ASCAP); page 68: "Stick to the Status Quo" by David N. Lawrence and
Faye Greenberg © 2005 Walt Disney Music Company (ASCAP); page 101: "When
There Was Me and You" by Jamie Houston © 2005 Walt Disney Music Company
(ASCAP); pages 130-132: "Breaking Free" by Jamie Houston © 2005 Walt Disney
Music Company (ASCAP)

This is a Parragon book

First published in 2006
Parragon
Queen Street House
4 Queen Street
Bath, BA1 1HE, UK

ISBN 1-40549-149-3
Printed in UK

It was a magical New Year's Eve at a vacation resort in the mountains. Gleaming white snow covered the ground, stars sparkled in the crisp, clear air, and everyone was beginning to get in the party mood.

Everyone, that is, except Troy Bolton and his father, Jack, who were still on the basketball court, playing one-on-one. They were covered with sweat, but they were having too much fun to stop.

Troy had the ball, and he was doing a good job of getting around his dad. After all, Troy was on the high school basketball team. Not only that, he was the team captain. He had the smooth moves and explosive action of a real star.

But Jack was more than just Troy's dad. Jack was also the basketball team's coach. So Mr. Bolton gave his son advice as they played.

"Keep working left, Troy," Mr. Bolton said. "The guy guarding you in the championship game won't expect that. You'll torch him."

Troy nodded, breathing hard. "By going left –" he said.

"He'll look middle, you take it downtown," his dad – and coach – explained.

Troy nodded again. "Like this?"

He spun past his father, jumped, and sunk a reverse layup. The ball whistled cleanly through the basket. Nothing but net!

His father grinned. "Sweet."

Troy grinned back. Nothing felt better than playing basketball when you were in the groove!

They could have played all night, but just then Troy's mum walked into the gym. She was wearing a sequined party dress and clearly had things other than B-ball on her mind.

"Boys? Hello?" she called. Once she got their attention, she went on. "Did we really fly all this way to play more basketball?"

Troy and his father glanced at each other slyly. They knew she didn't really want an answer to that question, but they gave her one anyway. In perfect unison, they shrugged and said, "Yeah."

Mrs. Bolton gave an exasperated sigh. "It's the last night of vacation. The party . . . ? Remember?"

Actually, they had both totally forgotten the big New Year's Eve party that the resort was holding, but they knew it wasn't wise to admit that.

"Oh, right, right," Mr. Bolton said quickly. "New Year's Eve." He hesitated, then asked, with some fear, "Do we have to wear funny hats?"

"Absolutely," she said firmly. "And we're due

in half an hour. Troy, they have a kids' party downstairs in the Freestyle Club."

"Kids' party?" Troy protested. That made him sound like a toddler!

"Young adults," his mum quickly amended. "Now go shower up."

With heavy sighs, Troy and his father did as she said.

As Troy took one last glance at the basketball court, he thought, The championship game is in a couple of weeks! I should be practising, not going to some stupid "kids' party"! Besides, how much fun could hanging out with a bunch of kids possibly be. . . .

Meanwhile, in another part of the lodge, another mother was about to tear her daughter away from a different fascinating activity.

Gabriella Montez was comfortably curled up in an overstuffed chair in the sitting area. She was enjoying the peace and quiet - everyone else was already at the party - and had totally lost herself in a book called *If You Only Knew Me*. It was the best book she had read since, well, since the last book she checked out of the library, and she couldn't wait to get to the end.

However, she didn't even get to the next page. The book was lifted right out of her hands, and she looked up to see her mother standing over her.

"Gabby, it's New Year's Eve," Mrs. Montez said. "Enough reading."

"But, Mum, I'm almost done and - " Gabriella protested.

Her mother just shook her head. "There's a teen party," she said firmly. "I've laid out your best dress. Go."

Gabriella eyed her mother's sparkly party dress and sighed. She knew when she was defeated.

She nodded, but asked, "Can I have my book back?"

Her mother handed it over and Gabriella headed toward her room to change. As soon as she was out of her mum's sight, however, she opened the book and began reading as she walked.

She might have to go to some stupid teen party, she thought, but she didn't plan to turn her brain off until the very last minute.

A short time later, Troy and Gabriella were in the teen club, feeling out of place. It was packed with kids wearing goofy party hats, blowing on noisemakers, and laughing.

Everyone else seems to be having fun, Troy thought glumly. He had showered and dressed in nice trousers and an ironed shirt, but he just wished he was back on the basketball court.

In another part of the room, Gabriella sat by herself, wearing the dress her mum had laid out. I could be back in my room, reading, Gabriella thought wistfully. I was just getting to the good part, too.

Neither one of them was having any fun at all.

Most of the kids in the room were watching a karaoke contest that was in full swing on a raised stage. As two teenagers finished their song, the MC called out cheerfully, "How about that for a couple of snowboarders?!"

The audience applauded, and the MC started looking around the room, trying to spot anyone else who was willing to sing karaoke to a room full of strangers. Spotlights swirled over the crowd, and the music played even louder to get the partygoers' adrenaline pumping.

"All right," the MC said into his mic. "Let's see who is gonna rock the house next. . . ."

That was the cue. The music stopped. The two spotlights picked out the next karaoke "volunteers."

One spotlight was on Troy.

The other was on Gabriella.

Both looked startled, and even a little terri- fied. They shook their heads, but it was no use. The MC jumped into the crowd and pulled them up onto the stage.

Troy and Gabriella were mortified. Somehow - they weren't quite sure how it happened -

microphones were put in their hands. There they were, stuck. Onstage. The centre of attention. And no way to escape.

Before either one of them could actually faint or throw up from fear, the music started.

Well, here goes, Troy thought with resignation. Might as well make the best of it . . .

He started singing, softly and carefully. He could barely get the words out. It was all he could do to read the lyrics on the screen of the karaoke machine and try to stay in tune. He sang:

"Livin' in my own world
Didn't understand
That anything can happen
When you take a chance"

No one seemed to be paying much attention to them. That was a *good* thing, Gabriella thought. And, after all, if this boy was willing to risk public humiliation, she might as well be a good sport and try to sing, too.

She opened her mouth and began singing. Although her voice was just above a whisper, it was sweet and pure. She sang:

"I never believed in
What I couldn't see
I never opened my heart
To all the possibilities"

All right, she thought. I can do this. It's not too terrible.

Okay, Troy thought. At least people aren't throwing things at us.

Still, they were too nervous to really belt out the song. They kept singing though, alternating the lines of the ballad.

Finally, they looked at each other, hoping for a little help from their partner in embarrassment. As they really saw each other, they both experienced something they never had before.

Troy felt a spark of electricity run over his skin. Gabriella felt a warm glow flood through her body. They smiled and, for the first time, began singing to each other. They sang more loudly, more boldly, with more self-assurance.

Suddenly, everyone in the room started to notice: there was something special going on up onstage! Kids began crowding around the edge of the stage, listening and swaying to the music. And now Troy and Gabriella were starting to enjoy themselves. Their nervousness was forgotten as they smiled into each other's eyes.

Before long, they were dancing across the stage and back again, as confident as if they were performing at an arena. As they moved to the music, they never took their eyes off each other.

When the song was over, the crowd applauded and cheered. Troy and Gabriella smiled, breathless and a little stunned by what had just happened.

Troy leaned over and said, "I'm Troy."

Gabriella nodded. "Gabriella."

Neither one of them could stop smiling. Both of them felt an excited, fizzy feeling inside, as if the world had just become a lot more fun.

CHAPTER TWO

They were still giddy from the excitement of their impromptu performance, so they went for a walk outside in the cold, sparkling air.

"You have an awesome voice," Troy said. "You're a singer, right?"

Gabriella shrugged. "Just the church choir is all." She smiled and admitted, "I tried to do a solo and nearly fainted."

"Why's that?" he asked, surprised.

She shook her head at the memory. "I took

one look at all the people staring only at me, and the next thing I knew, I was staring at the ceiling. End of solo career."

"The way you sang just now, that's hard to believe," he said sincerely.

"This is the first time I've done something like this," she answered.

Troy knew how she felt. "Completely," he agreed.

"You sound like you've done a lot of singing, too," she said.

"Oh, sure, lots," he said jokingly. "My showerhead is very impressed with me."

At that moment, everyone around them started chanting in unison: "Ten! Nine! Eight! . . ."

The New Year's Eve countdown had begun.

Troy and Gabriella glanced at each other, then just as quickly looked away.

"Seven! Six! Five! Four! . . ."

This was a magical night, Gabriella thought, wishing it would last longer.

I can't believe I didn't want to come to this party! Troy thought. This was awesome!

"Three! Two! One!"

Everyone began cheering and blowing on their noisemakers. Fireworks burst in the sky in showers of red, gold, and blue. Everyone was celebrating - but Troy and Gabriella were suddenly feeling awkward.

People kiss each other on New Year's Eve, Troy thought. Should I - ?

It's a tradition to kiss when the clock strikes midnight, Gabriella thought. Will he - ?

Neither one moved. After a few seconds, she smiled and said, "I guess I'd better go find my mum and wish her Happy New Year."

Troy nodded. The spell was broken, and he was a little relieved. "Me, too," he said. "I mean, not *your* mum - my mum . . . and dad. I'll call you tomorrow."

He pulled out his mobile, quickly snapped a picture of her, then handed her the phone.

"Put your number in."

Gabriella grabbed her own phone and handed it to him. "You, too – "

They quickly switched phones and tapped in their numbers. Then Gabriella turned to leave. Troy stopped her.

"Singing with you was the most fun I've had this vacation," he said sincerely. "Where do you – "

Another series of fireworks exploded overhead, drowning out whatever he was saying.

Gabriella was already at the stairs. She waved back, smiling, then vanished. Troy stood absolutely still, gazing after her.

A week later, school had started again at East High School in Albuquerque, New Mexico. It was the first morning back after winter vacation, and the scene was bedlam. Kids were piling out of buses, yelling at each other, showing off new clothes.

As Troy entered the courtyard, under the banner that read "Happy New Year, Wildcats," other students gave him high fives, low fives, and side fives.

His friend and basketball teammate Chad came up to him, yelling, "Yo, doggie! Troy, my hoops boy!"

Chad had wild, curly hair and a wired attitude to match. He was the loyal number two to Troy's number one and, before Troy could blink, he found that Chad had drawn in all the other members of the team. They were happy to see him, excited to be back together, and totally keyed up about the championship game, now just a couple of weeks away.

"Hey, Chad," Troy said. He waved at the other players. "Dudes . . . Happy New Year."

"Oh, yes, it will be a Happy Wildcat New Year," Chad shouted. "Because in two weeks we are going to the championships, with *you* leading us to infinity and beyond!"

Troy laughed, and the other members of the Wildcat basketball team nodded and high-fived each other. Chad was right. They were about to fulfill their destiny!

At that moment, Sharpay and Ryan Evans

pushed their way through the basketball posse. Both of them tossed their hair as only copresidents of the Drama Club could.

As usual, Sharpay looked Barbie-doll perfect, with blown-out hair, full makeup, and fashionable clothes. Her brother, Ryan, looked just as hip.

Zeke, one of the basketball players, watched Sharpay as she haughtily pushed her way through the crowd. "Hey, the ice princess has returned from the North Pole," he muttered to his crew.

"Yeah, she probably spent the holidays the way she always does," Chad said.

Jason, another basketball player, willingly filled the role of straight man. "How's that?" he asked.

"Shopping for mirrors!" Chad cracked.

He howled like a wolf in appreciation of his own joke. His teammates joined in.

Still howling, they walked by Taylor McKessie, the president of the Chemistry Club, who was accompanied by a few of her brainiac friends.

Taylor scornfully eyeballed the basketball players, then said to her friends, "Ah, behold the zoo animals heralding the new year. How tribal."

As her friends haughtily agreed, the bell rang and everybody hurried to their homerooms.

The crowds had thinned somewhat as Principal Matsui walked down the hall, escorting a new student. It was a nervous Gabriella and her mother, who were trying to listen as the principal gave them his sales pitch.

"We're consistently rated in the top ten academically in the state, and I think you'll also find this a wonderful community atmosphere," Principal Matsui said.

Gabriella tried to smile as she peeked in a window in a classroom door. The scene inside was total, first-day-back-at-school chaos. Her stomach flipped over and she cast an appealing look at her mother.

"Mum, my stomach - "

" - is always nervous on the first day at a new

school," her mother finished reassuringly. "You'll do great, you always do. And I've made my company promise that I can't be transferred again until you graduate."

Gabriella smiled weakly. This was always the worst part, she reminded herself.

"Worry not, Gabriella," Principal Matsui said. "I've reviewed your impressive transcripts. I expect your light will shine very brightly here at East High."

Gabriella knew he was trying to be helpful, but her stomach twisted even more at these words. "I don't want to be the school freaky genius girl again," she whispered to her mum.

Mrs. Montez hugged her. "Just be Gabriella," she said warmly.

Gabriella went to her homeroom with Ms. Darbus, the school's drama teacher. True to her theatrical background, she was flamboyantly dressed in a long, flowing dress and wore over-sized glasses.

Gabriella quickly took her seat, doing her best

to be invisible. She didn't see Troy enter with his best bud, Chad - but as Troy said hello to other students, he caught a glimpse of her from the corner of his eye.

Surprised, he craned his neck for a better look, but other students kept getting in the way. That girl, he thought. She looked just like - but what would the girl from New Year's Eve be doing here. . . ?

Before he could get a better look, the final bell rang and everybody scrambled to sit at their desks.

Ms. Darbus stood in front of the class as if she were taking centre stage in a Broadway theatre. "I trust you all had splendid holidays," she said. "Check the sign-up sheets in the lobby for new activities, especially our winter musical. There'll be single auditions for the supporting roles, as well as pairs auditions for our two leads - "

Chad looked around at his basketball team-mates, grinned, and blew a raspberry at the mention of the musical.

Ms. Darbus glared at him. "Mr. Danforth, this is a place of learning, not a hockey arena," she snapped.

Troy was still craning his neck, trying to see the new girl who looked so much like Gabriella. Finally, frustrated, he pulled his mobile from his pocket and thumbed through the menu.

The photo of Gabriella that he took on New Year's Eve popped up on the screen. He stared at it, remembering that magical night, as Ms. Darbus happily burbled on.

"There is also a final sign-up for next week's Scholastic Decathlon Competition," she said. "Chem Club president Taylor McKessie can answer your questions on that."

Meanwhile, Troy hit the SEND button on his phone. Suddenly, Gabriella's phone started ringing wildly. At first, she didn't even react. After all, who would be calling her?

Sharpay and Ryan grabbed for their phones. After all, wouldn't *every* call be for them?

Ms. Darbus strode to the front of the room,

the light of battle in her eyes. "Ah, the cell phone menace returns to our crucible of learning!" she cried. She grabbed a plastic bucket labelled "Cell-itary Confinement" and held it out to the brother and sister. "Sharpay and Ryan, your phones please, and I'll see you in detention."

They rolled their eyes, but deposited their phones in the bucket. The ringing, however, went on.

Ms. Darbus's gaze swept the room, searching for the source of the nefarious ring. Blushing, Gabriella fumbled in her backpack. As she finally dug her phone out and started to turn it off, she saw . . . Troy Bolton's photo?

Her eyes widened with surprise and she accidentally hit ANSWER instead of END.

Now Troy was staring in surprise at his phone, where he saw Gabriella's photo. But Ms. Darbus was looming over Gabriella and holding out her plastic bucket.

"We have zero tolerance on cell phones during

class," the drama teacher said sternly. "So, we'll get to know each other at detention. Phone, please . . . and welcome to East High, Miss Montez."

As she walked back to the front of the class, she saw Troy holding his phone and held out her bucket. "Mr. Bolton, I see your phone is involved. Splendid, we'll see you in detention, as well."

Troy sighed and dropped his phone in the bucket.

Behind him, Chad protested. "That's not even a possibility, Ms. Darbus, your honour, because we have basketball practice and Troy is - "

Ms. Darbus whirled around and glared at him. "That's fifteen minutes for you, too, Mr. Danforth. Count 'em!"

At the back of the class, Taylor smirked and whispered to one of her brainiac friends, "That could be tough for Chad, since he probably can't count that high."

She should have known better. Ms. Darbus had better hearing than a bat.

"Taylor McKessie," she said sharply. "Fifteen minutes."

Taylor's jaw dropped. She had never had to serve a minute of detention in her entire life!

But it was no use protesting. Ms. Darbus had already whirled around to survey the rest of the class. "Shall the carnage continue? Vacation is over, people. Way over! Any more comments? Questions?"

Jason, one of the basketball players, thought it was about time to restore a good mood to this morning's homeroom. He raised his hand and asked sincerely, "So how were your holidays, Ms. Darbus?"

As everyone looked at him in disbelief, the bell rang. The class bolted for the door, relieved to be free of Darbus rule for the time being.

CHAPTER THREE

Troy waited anxiously in the hall outside Ms. Darbus's homeroom, hanging back as his friends went on to their next classes.

Finally, Gabriella came out, and he walked towards her, hardly able to breathe.

When Gabriella saw him, her eyes widened in disbelief.

She said, "I don't - "

" - believe it," Troy finished in a whisper.

Gabriella nodded. "Me - "

" - either," Troy finished again. "But how . . ."

"My mum's company transferred her here to Albuquerque," Gabriella explained. She shook her head in disbelief. "I can't believe you live here. I looked for you at the lodge on New Year's Day, but - "

"We had to leave first thing," Troy said, still whispering.

Gabriella looked puzzled. "Why are you whispering?"

He looked a little embarrassed. "Oh, well, my friends know I went snowboarding, but I didn't tell them about the . . . singing . . . thing."

"Too much for them to handle?" she asked knowingly.

"It was . . . cool," Troy said quickly. He didn't want her getting the idea that he hadn't liked their singing debut! "But, my friends - that's not what I do. That was like a . . . different person."

They had reached the lobby, where activity

sign-up sheets were posted. Troy pointed at the sheet for the winter musical auditions.

"Now that you've met Ms. Darbus, I'll bet you can't wait to sign up for that," he said grinning.

Gabriella laughed. "I won't be signing up for *anything* here for a while," she said. "I just want to get to know the school." She glanced at him shyly. "But if you signed up, I'd consider coming to the show."

Troy shook his head. He couldn't even imagine the reaction he'd get if he signed up for the high school musical! "That's completely impossible," he said.

From behind him, Sharpay's voice said sweetly, "What's impossible, Troy? I wouldn't think 'impossible' is even in your vocabulary." As they turned to look at Sharpay, she gestured toward Gabriella. "So nice of you to show our new classmate around."

She raised one eyebrow as she saw Gabriella looking at the musical sign-up sheet. Very deliberately, Sharpay stepped in front of

Gabriella and signed her name with a flourish.

In fact, Gabriella noticed, Sharpay's signature took up the entire sign-up sheet!

But Sharpay looked at her, the picture of innocence, and said, "Oh . . . were you going to sign up, too? My brother and I have starred in all of the school's productions, and we really welcome newcomers." She smiled, ever so sweetly, then added, "There are a lot of supporting roles in this show. I'm sure we could find something for you."

"No, no," Gabriella said hastily. "I was just looking over the bulletin board. Lots going on at this school. Wow." I'm babbling, she thought. I have to stop it! Now! She pointed to Sharpay's huge signature. "Nice penmanship," she added weakly, before hurrying away to her next class.

Now that Sharpay had been left alone with Troy, she decided to seize the opportunity. "So, Troy," she said coyly, "I missed you during vacation. What'd you do?"

He shrugged. "Practised basketball. Snow-boarding. More basketball."

Sharpay nodded cheerfully and, using all of her dramatic training to sound as if she really cared, asked, "When's the big game?"

"Two weeks." Troy sounded resolute, deter-mined. Two weeks until we're either champions - or we're not, he thought.

"You're so dedicated," Sharpay said, batting her eyelashes just a bit. After a moment, she added, "Just like me. I hope you'll come watch me in the musical? Promise?"

Just like Sharpay to bring the conversation back to herself, Troy thought wryly. But he smiled and nodded as he walked away.

A few hours later, Troy and the basketball team had gathered in the gym for practice. Troy and Chad challenged each other by running a pres-sure drill, while the other boys ran a weave drill.

"Hey, you know that school-musical thing?"

Troy asked as he tried to get around Chad. "Is it true you get extra credit just for auditioning?"

"Who cares?" Chad asked as he blocked Troy.

Troy raised one eyebrow and tried to scoot around Chad from the other side. "It's good to get extra credit . . . for college and all," he said, trying to sound casual.

Chad laughed and shook his head. "Do you think LeBron James or Shaquille O'Neal ever auditioned for their school musical?" he asked mockingly.

"Maybe . . ." Troy said hesitantly.

"Troy, the music in those shows isn't hip-hop or rock or anything essential to the culture," Chad explained patiently. "It's like . . . *show music*. Costumes, makeup." He shuddered. "Frightening."

Troy shrugged, still trying to sound like it was no big deal. "I thought it might be a good laugh. Sharpay is kind of cute, too."

Now Chad looked at him with total disbelief. "So is a mountain lion, but you don't pet them."

Troy nodded, and gave up for the moment. Time to take charge of this practice, he thought. Time to focus. The championship game, he reminded himself sternly, is only weeks away.

He turned to his team. "All right, let's kick it in, run the shuffle drill," he yelled.

The team quickly took their positions and began bouncing basketballs and weaving around one another with the ease developed through hours of practise.

The balls began to bounce and the players began to move across the floor with a rhythmic, percussive movement. And Troy began to call out the practise drills.

"Coach said to
Fake right
And break left
Watch out for the pick
And keep an eye on defense
You gotta run the give and go
And take the ball to the hole

But don't be afraid
To shoot the outside 'J' "

The Wildcats had developed a team motto, and now Troy shouted it out to get his boys pumped up:

"Just keep ya' head in the game
Keep ya' head in the game
Just keep ya' head in the game
Don't be afraid to shoot the outside 'J' "

The team members smiled and moved even faster, smoother, better. Troy was a great captain, and he could motivate them like no one else!

Troy grabbed a ball and joined the drills, dribbling left around one player and right around another, still calling out drills.

When practice ended, everyone took deep breaths, smiling at how great they felt and how great they had looked. The Wildcats were definitely good to go for the championship!

CHAPTER FOUR

The next morning, Gabriella sat at a station in the chemistry lab, across the table from Taylor and next to Sharpay. The students were wearing neat white lab coats and busily setting up equipment as the chemistry teacher wrote equations on the blackboard.

Sharpay gave Gabriella a fake smile. Ever so casually, she said, "So, it seemed like you knew Troy Bolton."

Gabriella glanced up briefly, but she was

distracted by the teacher, who was solving the equation on the board. "Not really . . . I just asked him for directions," she said, even as she started checking the teacher's work on her scratch pad.

Sharpay raised the wattage of her smile just a bit. "Troy usually doesn't . . . interact . . . with new students."

"Why not?" Gabriella asked, not really listening. She looked at her equation. Hmmm. Her calculation was quite different from the teacher's. Should she say something? Maybe not. People didn't like it when you pointed out their mistakes. . . .

"It's pretty much basketball 24/7 with him," Sharpay said with a little laugh.

Now Gabriella wasn't listening to Sharpay at all. She rechecked her own calculation and murmured, "Pi to the eleventh power."

She thought she had said it quietly, but apparently not quietly enough.

The chemistry teacher turned around. "Yes, Miss Montez?"

"Oh, I'm sorry," Gabriella said, flustered. "I was just - "

Before she could finish her sentence, the teacher was standing by her chair, looking down at her notebook.

"Pi to the eleventh power?" the teacher said in surprise. "That's quite impossible." Then she whipped out a calculator and started punching in numbers. Across the table, Taylor had her calculator out as well, and was matching the teacher, keystroke for keystroke.

There was a brief, stunned pause. Then the teacher said, "I stand corrected." She turned back to the blackboard to revise her work. Then she looked over her shoulder, smiled warmly at Gabriella, and added, "And welcome aboard."

Gabriella blushed as Taylor stared at her, impressed.

Troy was strolling through the lobby on the way to his next class, when he caught sight of the musical audition sign-up sheet. His steps slowed.

It was crazy, he *knew* it was crazy, but he couldn't seem to stop thinking about the musical. He stood still, almost hypnotized by the piece of paper. He was so lost in his thoughts that he didn't notice Sharpay's brother, Ryan, who was hanging out nearby with a couple of the Drama Club kids.

Ryan's eyes narrowed suspiciously. When Troy finally moved on, Ryan ran up to the sheet, just to make sure. . . .

At that moment, Sharpay arrived. Ryan rushed up to her, breathless. "Troy Bolton was looking at our audition list!" he reported.

Sharpay stiffened, all senses suddenly alert. "Again? He was hanging around with that new girl, and they were both looking at the list." She paused a moment to think. "There's something freaky about her," Sharpay decided. "Where did she say she was from?"

Minutes later, Sharpay and Ryan were in the school library, doing an Internet search on

Gabriella. A number of newspaper articles immediately popped up on the screen.

"Whiz Kid Leads School to Scholastic Championship," read one headline.

"Sun High Marvel Aces Statewide Chemistry Competition," another headline said.

A photo of Gabriella showed her beaming into the camera and holding a number of awards.

As Sharpay printed out the article, Ryan said, "Whoa . . . an Einstein-ette. So why is she interested in our musical?"

"I'm not sure that she is," Sharpay said. "And we needn't concern ourselves with amateurs." She neatly folded the printouts and stood up. "*But* there's no harm in making certain that Gabriella is welcomed into school activities that are . . . appropriate . . . for her. After all, she loves pi."

And Ryan, who was always at least one step behind Sharpay, saw his sister's smile and knew that she had a plan.

Later that day, everyone who had been given detention had to serve their time.

Ms. Darbus, of course, held her detention on the stage of the school's theatre. The detainees' punishment was painting scenery, mopping the stage, and binding scripts.

Sharpay satisfied her requirements by telling Ryan how to paint a prop - and watching as he did it. Chad was trying to assemble a piece of scenery, but he was hopeless. All his agility and finesse on the basketball court translated to total clumsiness when he picked up a hammer. Troy and Gabriella were working on opposite sides of the stage, exchanging shy glances and trying to muster the courage to actually speak to each other.

Before either one of them could seize the moment, however, Taylor entered the auditorium and made a beeline for Gabriella. Taylor looked as if she had just won the lottery - and, considering that she was the Scholastic Club president, maybe she had.

She came to a halt in front of Gabriella and said, beaming, "The answer is yes!"

"Huh?" Gabriella was lost.

"Our Scholastic Decathlon team has its first competition next week, and there's certainly a chair open for you," Taylor said excitedly. She reached into her purse and pulled out a sheaf of newspaper articles about Gabriella's academic achievements.

Gabriella was stunned. "Where did those come from?"

"Didn't you slip them in my locker?" Now Taylor was confused.

"Of course not." Gabriella was more than confused - she was upset. She had wanted to pass for average, well, as close to average as she could. Now that plan was destroyed.

Sharpay stood to one side, pretending not to listen even as she listened as hard as she could.

Taylor quickly regrouped. "Well, we'd love to have you on the team. We meet almost every day after school." Then she had a quick flash of how much better their team would be if Gabriella joined, and added, "Please?"

"I need to catch up on the curriculum here before I think about joining any clubs . . ." Gabriella started hesitantly.

Sharpay whipped around. If there was any time to join this conversation, she thought, it was now. "But what a perfect way to get caught up, meeting with the smartest kids in the school. What a generous offer, Taylor!"

Gabriella looked from one girl to the other, feeling trapped. She was saved by Ms. Darbus, who walked onto the stage from the wings and said, "So many new faces in here today." She stared at them meaningfully. "I hope it doesn't become a habit, though the Drama Club can always use an extra hand. Now, as we work, let's probe the mounting evils of cell phones. My first thought on the subject is – "

Chad could recognize the beginning of a boring, long-winded lecture when he heard one. He quickly tried to hide inside a fake tree.

No luck. He could still hear Ms. Darbus, droning on. . . .

As Ms. Darbus listed all the problems with mobiles, the basketball team was taking the court for after-school practice. Coach Bolton entered and blew his whistle for practice to start.

"Okay, let's get rolling. Two weeks to the big - "

Then he paused and looked around. Something was wrong, he thought. Something was missing. Someone was missing. . . .

"Where are Troy and Chad?"

"Perhaps the most heinous example of cell-phone abuse is ringing in the theatre," Ms. Darbus was saying. "What temerity! For the theatre is a temple of art, a precious cornucopia of creative energy . . ."

Only Ryan and Sharpay were still listening. They nodded soberly in agreement.

Chad was now asleep inside the fake tree. He was even snoring.

Just as everyone thought they might faint from boredom, Coach Bolton ran into the auditorium, the light of battle shining in his eyes.

"Where's my team, Darbus?!" he yelled. "And what the heck are they doing here!?"

Ms. Darbus pulled herself to her full height and said icily, "It's called crime and punishment . . . Coach Bolton." She swept her arm toward the stage and added, "And proximity to the arts is cleansing for the soul."

Unfortunately, Chad chose that moment to suddenly wake up and fall out of his fake tree.

Coach Bolton held his temper and said to Ms. Darbus, as quietly as he could, "May we have a word?" He pointed to Troy and Chad and snapped, "You two, into the gym. Right now."

Troy and Chad jumped up, overjoyed at their sudden release from prison. As they dashed for the door, Troy reached into the bucket and grabbed his mobile.

And then they were gone. Gabriella had watched them the whole way.

* * *

Principal Matsui sat behind his desk, looking with resignation at the school's basketball coach and drama teacher. The coach was angry. The drama teacher was defiant. And Principal Matsui was starting to get that familiar feeling of heartburn. . . .

"If they have to paint sets for detention, they can do it tonight, not during my practice," the coach said.

Ms. Darbus appealed to the principal's sense of fair play. "If these were theatre performers instead of athletes, would you seek special treatment?"

"Darbus, we are days away from the biggest game of the year," Coach Bolton said, exasperated.

"And we are in the midst of auditions for our winter musical, as well," the drama teacher shot back. "This school is about more than young men in baggy shorts flinging balls for touchdowns."

"Baskets," the coach said through gritted teeth. "They shoot baskets."

Principal Matsui sighed wearily. "Listen, guys, you've been having this argument since . . . let me think . . ." He raised his voice. ". . . *since the day you both started teaching here!*" In a more reasonable tone, he added, "We are one school, one student body, one faculty. Can we not agree on that?"

The coach and drama teacher stared at him in disbelief. Clearly, they weren't going to agree on anything.

The principal shook his head and picked up a minibasketball from his desk. He tossed it toward the small basketball hoop on his wall and asked, "How's the team looking, anyway? Troy got them whipped into shape?"

Ms. Darbus could only roll her eyes.

Having won his latest skirmish with Ms. Darbus, Coach Bolton returned to the gym. He paced in front of his team and reminded them of the sad truth they all knew. "The West High Knights have knocked us out of the playoffs three years running. Now we're one game away from taking the championship right back from them."

He stopped to look directly at each player in turn. "It's time to make our stand. The team is you, and you are the team. And the team doesn't exist unless each and every one of you is fully focused on our goal."

He focused on Troy and Chad, and added meaningfully, "Am I clear?"

They nodded, as the whole team erupted into their cheer. "Wildcats! Getcha head in the game!"

Coach Bolton nodded, satisfied. They were pumped up. They were ready. And they were going to win!

Ms. Darbus's detention was over, and Taylor and Gabriella were finally free. As they walked across the courtyard together, Taylor said, "We've never made it out of the first round of the Scholastic Decathlon. You could be our answered prayer."

Gabriella smiled. She was flattered, but she

didn't budge. "I'm going to focus on my studies this semester and help my mum get the new house organized. Maybe next year."

"But - " Taylor began.

Gabriella searched her mind for some way to change the subject, and immediately thought of a topic she was most curious about. "What do you know about Troy Bolton?"

"Troy?" Taylor raised her eyebrows in surprise. "I wouldn't consider myself an expert on that particular subspecies." Six cheerleaders were approaching them, walking in a pack, as usual. Taylor's eyes sparkled with mischief as she added, "However, unless you speak cheerleader, as in - " She put on an enthusiastic, cheerleader voice and said breathlessly, "'*Isn't Troy Bolton just the hottie superbomb?*'"

On cue, the cheerleaders nodded and squealed enthusiastically.

"See what I mean?" Taylor said to Gabriella.

Gabriella laughed. "I guess I wouldn't know how to speak cheerleader."

Taylor nodded, happy to have made her point. "Which is why we exist in an alternative universe to Troy-the-basketball-boy."

Gabriella nodded. She knew that Taylor was right. In every high school, there were the brainiacs, the jocks, the band kids, the cheerleaders, the slackers . . . And every group was its own clique. No one ever moved from one clique to another. No one.

Still . . .

"Have you tried to get to know him?" she asked.

Taylor just laughed. "Watch how it works in the cafeteria tomorrow when you have lunch with us. Unless you'd rather sit with the cheerleaders and discuss the importance of firm nail beds."

"My nail beds are history," Gabriella said, smiling as she held up her hands to illustrate her point.

Taylor laughed and held up her hands in turn. Her nails looked just as bad as Gabriella's.

"Sister!" she cried, and they slapped hands in brainiac solidarity.

It was almost dark, but Troy was still in his backyard, shooting hoops. His father watched approvingly; his boy had moves, he thought. Good moves. Great moves, in fact.

He had to make sure Troy didn't lose focus. Not now.

"I still don't understand this detention thing," he said.

"It was my mess-up," Troy answered quickly, hoping this wouldn't turn into a big discussion. "Sorry, Dad."

"Darbus will grab any opportunity to bust my chops, and yours, too," his father reminded him.

Troy nodded, but his mind was on other things. After a moment, he asked hesitantly, "Dad, did you ever think about trying something new but were afraid of what your friends might think?

"You mean working on going left?" his dad asked. "You're doing fine."

Troy sighed but tried again. "I meant - what if you try something really new and it's a disaster, and all your friends laugh at you?"

"Then maybe they're not your friends," his father said. "That was my whole point about 'team' today. You guys have to look out for each other. And you're their leader."

"Yeah, but - " Troy was getting frustrated. He was really confused here, what with Gabriella and the musical and the way he had felt singing with her, and all his dad could think about was the basketball game.

"There are going to be college scouts at our game next week, Troy," his father said, as if Troy needed reminding. "Do you know what a scholarship is worth these days?"

"A lot?" Troy said. He didn't need to ask. He knew that a basketball scholarship could pay for four years of college. It would really help his parents financially. And it would help set him up for the future.

His father nodded. "Focus, Troy."

And Troy nodded in agreement. That's what he had to do. Focus. Concentrate on basketball. Don't think about anything else – not even singing.

Especially not singing.

CHAPTER FIVE

The next morning, Troy entered his homeroom class. The first person he saw was Gabriella. He sneaked a peek at her and realized she was looking at him, too. They both smiled sheepishly and looked away as Ms. Darbus said sternly, "I expect we learned our homeroom manners yesterday, people, correct?"

Everyone nodded obediently.

"If not, we have dressing rooms that need painting," she warned. "Now, a few

50

announcements. This morning during free period is your chance for musical auditions, both singles and pairs. I'll be in the theatre until noon, for those bold enough to explore the wingspan of their latent creative spirit."

Behind Troy, Chad rolled his eyes at this and leaned forward to whisper, "What time is she due back on the mother ship?"

His buddies snickered. Troy smiled uncomfortably. As he sat through the rest of homeroom, he tried to focus. Basketball, he kept saying to himself. Keep your eye on the prize, Troy. Don't think about anything except basketball.

When Ms. Darbus released the class, everyone piled out into the hallway. Chad quickly caught up with Troy. "Hey, Troy . . . the whole team's hitting the gym during free period. What are you going to have us run?"

Troy looked shifty. "Can't make it. I've got to catch up on homework."

Chad did a double take. "What?! Hello, this is only the second day back, dude," he protested.

"I'm not even behind yet, and I've been behind on homework since preschool."

Troy smiled and shrugged. "Catch you later," he said, then melted away in the crowd.

Chad looked after him, puzzled. "Homework?" he asked himself. "No way." He followed Troy, determined to figure out this mystery.

Chad would never make a good spy, Troy thought, catching a glimpse of his buddy out of the corner of his eye. He saw an open classroom door and quickly ducked inside. He saw Chad peer inside, and started talking to a couple of students as a cover. Then someone passing in the hall called out to Chad. As soon as Troy saw that his friend was distracted, he slipped out the back door of the classroom, scooted down the hall, and hurried down a stairwell.

The stairwell led outside to the courtyard. As Troy darted across the open area, he suddenly saw his father walking toward him. Thinking fast, Troy hid behind a wall, then opened the door to the automotive shop. He slipped inside just as his father approached.

Funny, Coach Bolton thought, I could have sworn I just saw Troy. . . . He looked around, but his son was nowhere in sight. The coach shrugged. I must be seeing things. Must be the pressure of the big game, he thought, and went on.

Troy's evasive skills and fast footwork came in handy as he moved quickly around the large pieces of equipment in the auto shop. As he reached the door, the auto-shop teacher approached.

". . . shortcut . . ." Troy explained quickly. ". . . late for class . . ." Then he ducked out the door, ran down the hall, and entered the school theatre from the backstage.

He peered out through the stage curtains and saw dozens of kids arriving, eager to try out. He spotted the caretaker's cart with a mop and bucket. He turned the mop upside down and used it as cover as he rolled the cart down a ramp, along the side of the theatre and into the shadows at the back of the auditorium.

From his safe hiding place, he watched as Ms. Darbus stepped onto the stage and began the auditions in her trademark dramatic style.

"This is where the true expression of the artist is realized, where inner truth is revealed through the actor's journey, where - " She stopped suddenly to glare around the theatre.

". . . WAS THAT A CELL PHONE?" she snapped.

Kelsi, the composer of this year's musical, was seated at a piano onstage. She answered Ms. Darbus timidly. "No, ma'am, it was the recess bell."

Ms. Darbus nodded, satisfied that her domain had not been invaded. "Those wishing to audition must understand that time is of the essence, we have many roles to cast, and the final callbacks will be next week. First, you'll sing a few bars, and then I will give you a sense of whether or not the theatre is your calling. Better to hear it from me than from your friends. Our composer, Kelsi Neilsen, will accompany you, and be available for rehearsals prior to callbacks. Shall we?"

She took a seat in the front row and braced herself for what was to come. She had too many years of experience with student auditions. She knew it wasn't going to be pretty.

The first student, a shy boy with a slightly flat voice, took the stage. Kelsi began playing the audition song, "What I've Been Looking For," and he sang along. When they'd finished, Ms. Darbus thought that it hadn't been *horrible*, but it certainly wasn't up to her high standards. Next came Susan, whose off-key voice and overly enthusiastic gestures were . . . well, Ms. Darbus thought, they were just scary bad. She winced as Susan belted out the song.

At the end of Susan's audition, Ms. Darbus put on a fake smile and said, "That's nice, Susan," adding, "perhaps best saved for a family gathering."

Then Alan bounded up, smiling. He was a very snappy dresser, but when he opened his mouth, Ms. Darbus realized sadly that he was a terrible singer.

She told him, "Alan, I admire your pluck. As to your voice . . . those are really nice shoes you're wearing. Next . . ."

Next was Cyndra, whose high-pitched wail made Ms. Darbus grimace. "Ah, Cyndra, what courage to pursue a note that's never been accessed in the natural world," she said, trying to be positive. "Bravo." She quickly corrected herself - after all, if there was one thing Ms. Darbus knew, it was theatre terminology. Bravo was said to congratulate a male singer, while brava was said to a female. "Brava!" she said to Cyndra. "How about . . . the spring musical?

She thought she had reached her breaking point, but that was before she saw the next audition, a boy and a girl who made strange gestures and performed slow somersaults as they chanted the lyrics in a hypnotic monotone.

"Okay . . ." Ms. Darbus finally said. "That was . . . just plain disturbing. Go see a counsellor."

As Troy watched the auditions wistfully, he felt a tap on his shoulder. It was Gabriella.

"Hey! You decided to sign up for something?" she asked.

"No," he answered. "You?"

She shook her head. "No." Then she took in his "disguise." "Why are you hiding behind a mop?"

Embarrassed, he awkwardly pushed the mop out of the way.

Gabriella looked at him knowingly. "Your friends don't know you're here, right?"

He hesitated, then admitted the truth. "Right." He glanced at the stage, where the auditions - and Ms. Darbus's putdowns - were continuing. "Ms. Darbus is a little . . . harsh."

"The Wildcat superstar is . . . afraid?" she teased him.

"Not afraid . . . just . . ." He hesitated again, then let his guard down. ". . . scared."

Relieved, Gabriella said, "Me, too." She looked at Ms. Darbus, who was dismissing yet another hopeful singer. "Hugely."

As they nervously watched Ms. Darbus, the teacher checked her clipboard and announced,

"For the lead roles of Arnold and Minnie, we only have one couple signed up." She smiled warmly at her star students. "Nevertheless, Ryan and Sharpay, I think it might be useful for you to give us a sense of why we gather in this hallowed hall."

This was just the moment Sharpay and Ryan were waiting for! They made grand entrances from opposite sides of the stage, and bowed to the almost-empty auditorium as if it were a Broadway theatre filled with a cheering audience.

Sharpay glared at Kelsi, who jumped as she realized that she was expected to clap for them. Quickly regrouping, Kelsi asked shyly, "What key?" and prepared to play.

But Ryan lifted a boom box and said smugly, "We had our rehearsal pianist do an arrangement." He hit the PLAY button, and he and his sister began their routine.

Their voices were great, Kelsi admitted to herself, and their dancing! They must have had a professional choreographer! But they had changed her soulful ballad into a fast, upbeat number. She couldn't help but feel disappointed as they sang.

They finished with a professional flourish and beamed proudly. They were good, and they knew they were good.

After that audition, everyone else knew it, too. The few kids who were gathering their courage to audition at the last minute quietly slinked out of the theatre, totally intimidated.

"Don't be discouraged!" Ryan called after them. "The theatre club doesn't just need singers, it needs fans, too! Buy tickets!"

Kelsi gathered her courage and approached Sharpay and Ryan. "Actually, if you do the part . . . with that particular song, I was hoping you'd – "

"*If* we do the part?" Sharpay interrupted her. "Kelsi, my sawed-off Sondheim, I've been in seventeen school productions. And how many times have *your* compositions been selected?"

"This is the first time," Kelsi admitted.

"Which tells us what?" Sharpay demanded.

Kelsi paused, not sure what answer was expected of her. "That I should write you more solos?"

Sharpay shook her head. "It tells us that you do *not* offer direction, suggestion, or commentary," she said condescendingly. "And you should be thankful that Ryan and I are here to lift your music out of its current obscurity. Are we clear?"

"Yes, ma'am," Kelsi said, thoroughly cowed. Then she caught herself. "I mean, Sharpay."

"Nice talking to you," Sharpay said in a tone of dismissal. She and Ryan turned on their heels and left with the regal stride of future superstars.

Kelsi began gathering her music, her pulse racing after this close encounter with celebrity ego.

"Okay, we're out of time, so if we have any last-minute sign-ups?" Ms. Darbus announced. She looked around the room. "No? Good. Done."

She tossed her clipboard into her shoulder bag and began to leave. Gabriella took a deep

breath. It was now or never, she thoug[...]
she could have second thoughts, she ran[...]
the drama teacher.

"I'd like to audition, Ms. Darbus."

Ms. Darbus shook her head. "Timeliness means something in the world of theatre, young lady. Plus, the individual auditions are long, long over. And there were simply no other pairs."

Then, out of the darkness, Troy's voice said, "I'll sing with her." He moved from the shadows to stand with Gabriella.

"Troy Bolton?" The drama teacher looked more than taken aback. She looked suspicious. "Where's your . . . sport posse, or whatever it's called?"

"Team," Troy said helpfully. "But I'm here alone. Actually," he smiled at Gabriella, "I'm here to sing with her."

"Yes, well, we treat these shows very seriously here at East High," Ms. Darbus sniffed.

"I called for the pairs audition, and you didn't

...he pointed to the clock. "Free period ...then, in an effort to sound gracious, ...said. "Next musical, perhaps."

As she headed for the back of the auditorium, Kelsi started to leave the stage, clutching her sheet music. She was so distracted by all the drama - on and off the stage - that she tripped over the piano leg and sprawled to the floor. Her pages of music scattered everywhere.

Troy jumped up onstage, lifted her up, and began helping her collect the papers. Kelsi didn't lift a finger to help - she was too stunned. Troy Bolton, the Troy Bolton, the school's star basketball player, was helping her? She stared at him, frozen.

Troy didn't notice the effect he was having on Kelsi. "You composed the song that Ryan and Sharpay just sang?" he asked.

Speechless, Kelsi nodded.

"And the entire show?" he asked.

Again, Kelsi managed to nod. Barely.

"That's way cool," he said, truly impressed. "I

can't wait to hear the rest of the show." When she didn't answer, he went on. "Why are you so afraid of Ryan and Sharpay? It's your show."

Kelsi was so startled, she actually blurted out a couple of words. "It is?"

"Isn't the composer of a show like the playmaker in basketball?" he asked.

"Playmaker?" Kelsi hadn't ever heard that term, but she liked the sound of it.

"The person who makes everyone else look good," he explained. "Without you, there *is* no show. You're the playmaker here, Kelsi."

"I am?" Kelsi had never thought of it that way before. But now that Troy Bolton - *the* Troy Bolton! - had said it, she had to admit, it made a certain kind of sense. Feeling bold and strong for the first time, she sat at the piano and asked, "Do you want to hear the way that duet is supposed to sound?"

She began playing the audition song that Ryan and Sharpay had rearranged. She played it more slowly, with feeling and soul. Troy and Gabriella listened with growing appreciation.

"Wow, now that's really nice," Troy said.

Kelsi pushed the music toward Troy.

He looked at it. Did he dare?

Gabiella looked at it, too, feeling tempted.

Then Troy began to sing softly:

"It's hard to believe
That I couldn't see
You were always there beside me"

Gabriella soon joined in, a little more boldly.

"Thought I was alone
With no one to hold"

When they sang together, the harmonies melded perfectly.

They both felt the same glow they had felt on New Year's Eve. Kelsi beamed as she listened to this simple, pure interpretation of her song. It was the way she had dreamed it would sound.

As they finished, Ms. Darbus stepped forward from the darkness by the back door. She had been watching and listening the entire time. And what she had seen and heard had surprised her.

As she wrote their names on her clipboard, she called out, "Bolton, Montez, you have a call-back. Kelsi, give them the duet from the second act. Work on it with them."

The bell rang. Ms. Darbus strode off to her next class as Troy and Gabriella looked at each other, totally stunned. Now what?

Kelsi handed them the music and said eagerly, "If you want to rehearse, I'm usually in the music room during free period and after school . . . and sometimes even during biology class."

All was quiet until the next morning. Then, Sharpay walked into school. She checked out the sheet that Ms. Darbus had posted, listing who had to take part in a second round of auditions. And she saw the dreaded phrase. . . .

"CALLBACK!!!" Her scream echoed through the halls of East High.

Ryan rushed to her side and read aloud from the sheet. " 'Callback for roles of Arnold and Minnie, next Thursday, 3:30 P.M. Ryan and Sharpay Evans. Gabriella Montez and Troy Bolton.' "

"Is this some kind of joke?" Sharpay demanded angrily. "They didn't even audition."

"Maybe we're being punked?" Ryan suggested. "Maybe we're being filmed right now. Maybe we'll get to meet Ashton!"

"Shut up, Ryan!" Sharpay snarled.

By this time, a crowd of students had gathered. Troy's teammates Chad, Jason, and Zeke were among the students staring at the list.

Chad saw Troy's name. An expression of complete and utter horror crossed his face. "WHAT?!!!!!" he yelled.

By lunchtime, the news that Troy and Gabriella had tried out for the musical had spread throughout the school. As students entered the cafeteria, they took their usual seats. Jocks sat with jocks. Brainiacs sat with brainiacs. Drama kids sat with drama kids. Skater dudes, cheerleaders, punks . . . each sat with their own kind.

That was the way the world was meant to be. Orderly. Predictable. Understandable.

Sharpay held court at the head of the drama kids table. Kelsi sat at the far end, listening to every word, but keeping quiet, as usual.

"How dare she sign up," Sharpay said. "I've already picked out the colours for my dressing room."

"And she hasn't even asked our permission to join the Drama Club," Ryan pointed out supportively.

"Someone's got to tell her the rules," Sharpay decided.

"Exactly," her brother agreed. He thought for a moment, then asked, "What are the rules?"

As if he was just waiting for that cue, Zeke, a tall, burly basketball player with a killer smile, began singing. The other jocks gathered around,

67

curious. Zeke looked at them, took a deep breath, and admitted, "If Troy admits he sings, then I can tell my secret." He whispered to them, "I bake."

"What?" Chad couldn't believe what he had heard.

But now that he had confessed, Zeke felt that he had been set free. "I love to bake," he said. "Scones, strudel, even apple pandowdy." He was too caught up in his enthusiasm to stop. "I dream of making the perfect crème brûlée," he said as Chad buried his face in his hands.

The jocks were horrified. Urgently, they sang:

"*No, no, no, nooooooooooooo*
Stick to the stuff you know
If you wanna be cool
Follow one simple rule
Don't mess with the flow, no no
Stick to the status quo"

Zeke had started something. Over at the brainiacs table, Martha Cox, a studious girl who wore glasses and a plain skirt and jumper, suddenly jumped up from the table, threw her arms wide and exclaimed, "Hip-hop is my passion! I love to pop, lock, break, and jam."

She demonstrated a few moves, and one of the brainiac boys got worried. "Is that legal?" he asked the table.

Martha turned to the worried boy and said, "It's just . . . dancing. And the truth is, sometimes I think it's even cooler than - " She took a deep breath, gathered her courage, and finished. " - homework!"

Her friends looked as if they were about to faint.

Meanwhile, across the cafeteria, a skateboarder stood up and confessed, "If Troy can be in a show, then I'm coming clean." He hesitated, then gave it up. "I play the cello."

"Awesome," said another skateboarder. "What is it?"

His friend mimed playing the cello, but saw only confusion in the other boarder's face.

"A saw?"

"No, it's like a giant violin," the first boarder explained.

"Do you have to wear a costume?" the second boarder asked.

"Tie and coat," the unmasked cello player said.

"That's uncalled for!" his friend exclaimed.

The spirit of rebellion was building, however! The skater dude jumped up on his table and enthusiastically mimed playing the cello. Brainiac Martha was busting out some cool hip-hop moves from the top of her table, dancing and swaying to the rhythm in her head.

The students who had confessed their secret loves were now all standing on their respective cafeteria tables as if they were on stages, singing their hearts out.

Finally, Sharpay had had enough! She shouted, "Everybody, quiet!" Her voice echoed through the room. All the students stopped and stared at Gabriella and Taylor, who had just entered the cafeteria and picked up their lunch trays.

Gabriella noticed the attention and said nervously, "Why are they pointing at you?"

"Not me," Taylor replied. "You."

"Because of the callback?" The memory of that horrible church choir experience flooded back into Gabriella's mind. "I can't have people stare at me. I really can't."

As Gabriella and Taylor wove through the crowd to a table, Gabriella stumbled. Her tray went flying and spilled chili fries, ketchup, and melted cheese all over . . . Sharpay.

Sharpay stood still, stone-faced, and Gabriella tried to clean the food from Sharpay's blouse. It only made the mess worse.

At that moment, Troy entered the cafeteria and noticed what was going on. He headed over to help Gabriella, but Chad quickly intercepted him. "You can't get in the middle of that, Troy," his buddy warned. "Far too dangerous."

He dragged Troy over to the safest place in the

room: their usual table. Troy looked around and realized that the cafeteria was buzzing with energy and excitement.

"What's up?" he asked.

"Oh, let's see," Chad answered. "You missed free-period workout yesterday to audition for some heinous musical. Suddenly people are . . . confessing. Zeke is baking . . . crème brûlée."

Troy frowned, trying to follow all this. This was a lot of confusing information, so he seized on the easiest point to clear up. Crème brûlée?

"What's that?"

"A creamy, custardlike filling with a caramelized surface," Zeke said, happy to finally be able to talk about his secret passion. "Very satisfying."

Chad rolled his eyes. This was getting out of control! "Shut up, Zeke!" he yelled. Then he turned to Troy. "Do you see what's happening? Our team is coming apart because of your singing thing. Even the drama geeks and brainiacs suddenly think they can . . . talk to us. The skater dudes are . . . mingling. People think they can suddenly . . . do other stuff! Stuff that's . . . *not their stuff*!"

He pointed dramatically to the kids sitting at Sharpay's table. "They've got you thinking about show tunes, when *we've* got a playoff game next week!"

At this moment, Ms. Darbus walked into the cafeteria and noted the unusual sense of turmoil among the students. She spotted Sharpay, who was trying, without success, to clean her blouse with a tissue.

"What happened here?" Ms. Darbus demanded.

"Look at this!" Sharpay cried indignantly. "That Gabriella girl dumped her lunch on me . . . on purpose! It's all part of their plan to ruin our musical."

She pointed an accusing finger at the jock table. "And Troy and his basketball robots are obviously behind it. Why do you think he auditioned?"

She sensed that she was convincing Ms.

Darbus that some sort of conspiracy was being hatched. She smiled a bit and went on smoothly, "After all the work you've put into this show, it just doesn't seem right."

Kelsi watched and listened as Sharpay worked on Ms. Darbus. But despite her new confidence, she still couldn't take on the queen of the Drama Club *and* Ms. Darbus.

At least, not yet.

Coach Bolton was eating a sandwich at his desk and reading the newspaper sports page, when Ms. Darbus suddenly barged in. He dropped the paper with a sigh - he had been having such a nice, peaceful lunch - as the drama teacher said, "All right, Bolton, cards on the table right now."

"Huh?" Sometimes Coach Bolton thought that all that make-believe was affecting Ms. Darbus's mind. She always seemed off in some other world, from what he could see.

"You're tweaked that I put your stars in detention, so now you're getting even?" Ms. Darbus was beside herself with rage.

"What are you talking about, Darbus?" The coach was honestly confused.

"Your 'all-star' son turned up for my audition," Ms. Darbus said. "I give every student an even chance, which is the long and honourable tradition of the theatre - something you wouldn't understand - but if he's planning some kind of practical joke in my chapel of the arts - "

The coach grasped the one truth he knew he could cling to amid this barrage of nonsense. "Troy doesn't even sing."

"Oh, you're wrong about that. But I won't allow my *Twinkle Town* musical made into a farce - "

He could help it. He almost laughed in her face, but managed to choke it back at the last second. "*Twinkle Town*?" he asked.

Apparently, his poker face wasn't as good as he thought. Ms. Darbus knew he was laughing, and immediately assumed that he had sent Troy to audition as some kind of practical joke.

"See!" she cried. "I knew it! I knew it!"

Back in the cafeteria, Taylor and Gabriella were still trying to recover from the chaos that had erupted.

"Is Sharpay really, really mad?" Gabriella asked. "I said I was sorry."

"No one has beaten out Sharpay for a musical since kindergarten," Taylor explained.

"I'm not trying to beat anyone out," Gabriella protested. "We weren't even auditioning. We were just . . . singing."

Taylor shook her head. "You won't convince Sharpay of that," she warned. "If that girl could figure out how to play both Romeo and Juliet, her own brother would be aced out of a job."

"I told you, it just . . . happened." Then she admitted the real truth. "But . . . I liked it. A lot."

She sighed and then asked Taylor the question she had been wondering about ever since New Year's Eve. "Do you ever feel like there's this whole other person inside of you, just looking for a way to come out?"

Taylor gave her a sharp look. "No," she said decisively.

The bell rang to signal the end of the lunch period. Sharpay stalked out of the cafeteria, but not before leveling a death-ray glance at Gabriella.

Then Zeke stepped up to stop Sharpay. He was fizzing with happiness, now that his secret love of baking was out in the open.

"Hey, Sharpay," he said. "Now that Troy's going to be in your show . . ."

"Troy Bolton is *not* in my show!" she snapped.

Zeke pushed on, undeterred. "I thought maybe you'd like to come to see me play ball some time. . . ."

Sharpay tossed her head and said grandly, "I'd rather stick pins in my eyes."

He frowned at her, puzzled. "Wouldn't that be awfully uncomfortable?"

She rolled her eyes in exasperation. "Evaporate, tall person!" she said as she stormed away.

Crestfallen, Zeke called after her, "I bake . . . if that helps."

The next day, Gabriella opened her locker and found a note. She read it quickly, then looked at a yellow door at the end of the hall. She was a little confused - and very intrigued.

She opened the door and found a staircase that led up to the roof. As she opened the door and stepped out into the beautiful, sunny day, she saw Troy sitting on a bench. He was surrounded by lush plants, all being grown as hydroponic experiments.

"So this is your private hideout?" she asked, smiling.

"Thanks to the Science Club," Troy said. "Which means my buddies don't even know about it."

Gabriella wondered about that. His teammates didn't seem to be his only buddies.

"Looks to me like everyone on campus wants to be your friend," she pointed out.

"Unless we lose."

He seemed a little down about that, she thought. The pressure must be intense, especially since . . .

"I'm sure it's tricky being the coach's son," she said.

Troy shrugged. "It makes me practise a little harder, I guess. I don't know what he'll say when he hears about the singing thing."

"You're worried?" She was surprised. Troy seemed so cool, so confident. Not the type to worry. Ever.

But Troy nodded. "My parents' friends are always saying, 'Your son is the basketball guy, you must be so proud.' Sometimes I don't want to be the basketball guy. I just want to be . . . a guy."

Gabriella smiled with understanding. He didn't want to be the basketball guy any more than she wanted to be genius girl. They were both so much more than that. . . .

"I saw how you treated Kelsi at the audition yesterday," she said softly. "Do your friends know *that* guy?"

He shook his head. "To them, I'm the play-maker dude."

"Then they don't know enough about you, Troy." Gabriella paused, then decided it was time to share a confession of her own. "At my other schools I was the freaky math girl. It's cool coming here and being . . . anyone I want to be. When I was singing with you, I just felt like . . . a girl."

"You even looked like one, too," he teased her.

She laughed, glad to have the seriousness of the moment lightened a bit. "Remember in kindergarten you'd meet a kid, know nothing about them, then ten seconds later were best friends, because you didn't have to be anything but yourself?"

"Yeah . . ." Troy's voice was wistful.

"Singing with you felt like that," Gabriella said sincerely.

"I never thought about singing, that's for sure," Troy said. "Until you."

"So you really want to do the callbacks?" she asked.

He thought about it for a moment as he looked at her. Really looked at her. Then he smiled. "Hey, just call me freaky callback boy."

She smiled, a glowing smile of pure happiness. "You're a cool guy, Troy. But not for the reasons your friends think." He looked down, a little embarrassed, and she moved on quickly. "Thanks for showing me your top secret hiding place. Like kindergarten."

Then the bell rang, breaking the mood and making Troy realize he was late. And that meant detention!

The next day, Kelsi sat alone at the piano, playing with passion and energy. No one else was in the room. Just Kelsi and her music. Exactly the way she liked it.

Troy sat in a stairwell, practising his audition song. He kind of liked the way his voice echoed.

At that moment, Ryan rounded a corner and slowed down to listen. He could have sworn he heard someone singing. . . .

Meanwhile, Gabriella had found her own private spot with great acoustics: the girls' bathroom. She stood in front of the mirror and sang.

Sharpay was heading for class when she thought she heard the faint sound of singing. She turned her head to spot where it was coming from . . . there! She opened the bathroom door and went in, looking everywhere for the source of the music.

She found . . . nothing.

I've been rehearsing too much, Sharpay thought as she left the bathroom. I'm starting to hear that music everywhere I go!

Gabriella stepped out of the hiding place she had quickly found for herself and smiled.

Later that day, in the school's rehearsal room, Kelsi played the piano for Gabriella and helped her with her phrasing.

Then it was Troy's turn. He worked as hard as he could, but singing was harder than he thought. Just when he was getting frustrated beyond belief, Kelsi would stop to encourage him.

Just like basketball, he thought. You've gotta keep practising.

And he started to sing again.

The other basketball players were in the gym, warming up for practice. Coach Bolton kept checking his watch. Where was Troy? He frowned. Something was going on with that boy. Something weird. Something different. And it was getting in the way of his championship dream.

Coach Bolton didn't like it. He didn't like it at all.

He would have liked it even less if he had known where Troy was.

In detention. Again.

The only bright side was that Gabriella was

there, too. They stole glances at each other as they painted scenery. Each one was smiling a secret smile. Each one was hearing the audition song in their heads.

Finally, detention was over. Troy raced into the gym - only to find that practice was over, too.

The players headed toward the locker room. Hoping to recover a bit from his absence, Troy said to his father, "I'm going to stay awhile, work on free throws."

Coach Bolton nodded coldly in agreement. "Since you were late for practice . . . again . . . I think your teammates deserve a little extra effort from you."

He gave Troy a hard look, then headed for his office.

Troy sighed. He started shooting baskets, sinking one after the other.

Then Gabriella poked her head around the door. He smiled in welcome and waved her in.

She entered cautiously, looking around with curiosity. "Wow, so this is your . . . real stage."

"I guess you could call it that," he said. "Or just a smelly gym."

He bounced the ball over to her. She grabbed it and took a shot. It went in, and Troy turned to her, surprised.

"Whoa . . . don't tell me you're good at hoops, too?"

"I once scored forty-one points in a league championship game," she said, straight-faced.

"No way," he said, impressed.

"Yeah," she laughed, "the same day I invented the space shuttle and microwave popcorn."

He laughed, stole the ball back from her, took a shot, and missed. She grabbed it on the rebound and said, "I've been rehearsing with Kelsi."

"I know," he said. "Me, too. And I was late for practice. So if I get kicked off the team, it'll be on your conscience."

Gabriella looked startled. "Hey, I - "

"Gabriella," Troy said, laughing. "Chill."

She gave him a stern look for the teasing just

85

as Coach Bolton came back to the gym.

"Miss, I'm sorry, this is a closed practice," the coach said, his voice booming in the empty gym.

"Dad, practice is over," Troy protested.

"Not until the last player leaves the gym," the coach said. "Team rules."

Gabriella sensed the tension between them and quickly said, "Oh, I'm sorry, sir."

"Dad, this is Gabriella Montez," Troy said.

Gabriella looked at the coach with interest. So this was Troy's father. . . .

The coach looked at her with disapproval. "Your detention buddy?" he said.

Okay. Gabriella knew when it was time to leave. "I'll see you later, Troy," she said. "Nice to meet you, Coach Bolton."

"You as well, Miss Montez," the coach said, as he gave her a stern look.

Troy faced his dad. "Detention was my fault, not hers."

"You haven't missed practice in three years," his father pointed out. "That girl turns up and you're late twice."

Troy felt anger flare up in his chest. "'That girl' is named Gabriella, and she's very nice," he said sharply.

"Helping you miss practice doesn't make her 'very nice,'" his dad said, just as sharply. "Not in my book. Or your team's."

"She's not a problem, Dad," Troy said, frustrated. Why was his father - why was his coach - making such a big deal about this? "She's just . . . a girl."

"But you're not just 'a guy,' Troy." His father - and his coach - was equally frustrated. "You're the team leader, so what you do affects not only this team, but the entire school. Without you completely focused, we won't win the game next week. And playoff games don't come along all the time . . . they're something special."

Without warning, a series of memories ran through Troy's mind: Singing with Gabriella. Laughing with Gabriella. Talking with Gabriella.

"A lot of things are special," he said.

"You're a playmaker, not a singer," his father reminded him.

Exasperated, Troy yelled, "Did you ever think maybe I could be both?" He turned abruptly and headed for the locker room.

His dad watched him go, worried. He hoped he had been able to get through to Troy, but he feared that he hadn't.

Inside the hall between the locker room and the gym, Chad, Jason, and Zeke huddled together. They had been listening, wide-eyed, to the confrontation between Troy and his father.

Now they looked at one another and shook their heads.

This was not good. This was not good at all.

CHAPTER SIX

The next day, Chad sat next to Troy at a study table in the library. Without even saying hello, he started right in with the question on his mind - not to mention the minds of everyone on the team.

"What spell has this elevated-IQ temptress-girl cast that suddenly makes you want to be in a musical?" he asked.

"I just . . . did it," Troy sighed. "Who cares?"

"Who cares?" Chad looked injured. "How about your most loyal best friend?"

The librarian glared at him. "Quiet in here, Mr. Danforth."

Chad pointed at Troy. "It's him, Miss Falstaff, not me." Chad turned back to Troy, his voice more urgent now. "You're a hoops dude, not a musical-singer person. Have you ever seen Michael Crawford on a cereal box?"

"Who is Michael Crawford?" Troy asked.

"Exactly my point," Chad said, vindicated. "He was the Phantom of the Opera on Broadway. My mum saw that musical twenty-seven times and put Michael Crawford's picture in our refrigerator. Not on it, *in* it. Play basketball, you end up on a cereal box. Sing in musicals, you end up inside my mum's refrigerator."

Troy frowned, trying to follow this logic. "Why did she put his picture in her refrigerator?"

"One of her crazy diet ideas," he said dismissively. "I do not attempt to understand the female mind, Troy. That's frightening territory."

He looked up to see the librarian heading in their direction. He leaned over and whispered,

"How can you expect the rest of us to be focused on the game if you're off somewhere in leotards singing in *Twinkle Town*?"

"No one said anything about leotards. . . ." Troy sounded a little worried.

Chad seized his advantage. "Maybe not yet, my friend, but just wait! We need you, Captain. Big-time."

Oops. The librarian was looming over them. "Mr. Danforth!"

Chad pointed to Troy again. "I tried to tell him, Miss Falstaff!" he said, the picture of innocence. To further the illusion, he turned to Troy and added, "I really tried!"

Then he crept away, followed by the librarian's accusing glare. Troy sat very still, thinking hard about what Chad had said.

Inside the chemistry lab, Taylor and the other members of the Scholastic Club were hard at work, when Chad, Jason, and Zeke entered.

Chad walked up to Taylor and said, "We need to talk."

The two groups were deep in conversation when Sharpay and Ryan passed the open door of the chemistry lab. They stopped to look and listen.

"Something isn't right," Sharpay said.

Ryan nodded. "They must be trying to figure out a way for Troy and Gabriella to actually beat us out. The jocks rule most of the school, but if they get Troy into the musical, then they've conquered the entire student body."

"And if those science girls get Gabriella hooked up with Troy Bolton, the Scholastic Club goes from drool to cool," Sharpay gasped. Her eyes narrowed. "Ryan, we need to save our show from people who don't know the difference between a Tony Award and Tony Hawk."

Back in the chemistry lab, Chad had finished making his pitch to Taylor and her team.

"You really think that's going to work?" Taylor

When they sang together, Troy and Gabriella forgot how nervous they were about performing in front of a crowd.

"This is the first time I've done something like this," said Gabriella.

**When the clock struck midnight, Troy thought,
'People kiss each other on New Year's Eve. Should I -?'**

**"We have zero tolerance on cell phones during class,"
said Ms. Darbus. "Welcome to East High, Miss Montez."**

When Gabriella saw Troy in the hallway,
her eyes widened in disbelief.

"I won't be signing up for anything here for a while,"
Gabriella said. "I just want to get to know the school."

"Oh . . . were you going to sign up, too?
My brother and I have starred in all of the school's
productions," Sharpay informed Gabriella.

"Troy, the music in those shows isn't hip-hop or rock
or anything essential to the culture," Chad said.

"Our Scholastic Decathlon team has its first competition next week and there's certainly a chair open for you," Taylor told Gabriella.

"This morning during free period is your chance for musical auditions," announced Ms. Darbus.

**"Why are you so afraid of Ryan and Sharpay?"
Troy asked Kelsi. "It's your show."**

**Sharpay and Ryan were a little too proud of
their audition.**

When Troy and Gabriella sang together at the audition, the harmonies melded perfectly.

"I never thought about singing, that's for sure," Troy said. "Until you."

"What spell has this elevated-IQ temptress-girl cast that suddenly makes you want to be in a musical?" Chad asked.

Gabriella's confidence grew as she sang with Troy at their callback audition.

asked. The other members of the Scholastic Club looked equally dubious.

"It's the only way to save Troy and Gabriella from themselves," Chad said with certainty.

Taylor looked at her team for their input. After a brief pause, they all nodded. After all, they needed Gabriella as much as the basketball team needed Troy.

"We start tomorrow," Chad said, satisfied.

The next morning, as students poured into the school, Chad looked around secretively, as if on a spy mission. He spotted Taylor across the courtyard and gave a quick nod, in the best secret agent style.

She rolled her eyes at his theatrics and met him in a corner.

"My watch says seven forty-five, mountain standard time," he said in a hushed tone. "Are we synched?"

Taylor never wore a watch. She had an infallible inner clock. "Whatever."

"Then we are on go mode for lunch period?" Chad asked. "Exactly 12:05?"

She nodded and handed him a small laptop with a video lens attached. "Yes, Chad," she said. "We're a go. But we're not Charlie's Angels, okay?"

He grinned. "I can dream, can't I?"

And they were off.

At exactly 12:05, the lunch bell rang. Dozens of students headed to the cafeteria for lunch, but Troy headed for the locker room.

He arrived to find his whole team waiting for him. As he stepped in the room, Jason closed the door behind him and stood in front of it, blocking it with his body.

Chad stood in the centre of the room next to a table covered with trophies and photos. He picked up one of the photos and held it up for Troy to see.

"'Spider' Bill Natrine, class of '99," Chad said. "MVP, league championship game."

He pointed to a trophy from that game.

Zeke held up the next photo.

"Sam Netletter, class of '02," he said. "Known far and wide as 'Sammy Slamma-Jamma.' Captain, MVP, league championship team."

He pointed to that trophy as Jason picked up the next photo.

" 'Thunderclap' Hap Haddon, '95," Jason said and pointed to the relevant trophy. "Led the Wildcats to back-to-back city championships. A legend."

"Yes, legends, one and all," Chad said, underlining the theme. "And do you think any of these Wildcat legends *became* legends by getting involved in musical auditions, just days before the league championship *playoffs*?"

The team stared intently at Troy and chanted in unison, "Getcha head in the game!"

"These Wildcat legends became legends because they never took their eye off the prize," Chad said. He was on a roll.

The team chanted again. "Getcha head in the game!"

Chad turned to the team and asked, "Now, who was the first sophomore ever to make starting varsity?"

The team smiled as one. "Troy!" they yelled.

Chad nodded. "So who voted him our team captain for *this* year?"

"Us!" the team yelled.

"And who is going to get their sorry butts kicked in Friday's championship game if Troy is worried about an audition?" Chad asked.

"We are," the team said together, depressed.

"Hey, there are twelve of us on this team," Troy protested. "Not just me."

Chad raised one eyebrow. "Just twelve? I think you're forgetting a very important thirteenth member of this squad - " He pulled out another photo.

It was a black-and-white photo of a kid in a basketball uniform. From the style of the uniform - and the style of the hair - it was clear this photo was old school.

Troy took a good look. His jaw dropped.

"That's my dad . . ." he whispered.

Chad propped the photo against an old trophy. "Yes, Troy, Wildcat basketball champion, class of 1981. Champion . . . father - and now coach. A winning tradition like no other."

Troy looked around at his team. What was going on? He felt as if his team was trying to deprogram him or something!

Meanwhile, Gabriella and the rest of the Scholastic Club had gathered in the chemistry lab with brown-bag lunches. Taylor was pointing to a series of photos and sketches on the dry-erase board. They showed the process of evolution, Taylor style.

She lectured, "From lowly Neanderthal and Cro-Magnon, to early warriors, medieval knights . . . all leading to . . ." She unscrolled the pièce de résistance, a full-length photo of an NBA player's body, with Troy's head superimposed on it. ". . . lunkhead basketball man! Yes, our culture worshipped the aggressor throughout the ages, and we end up with spoiled, overpaid, bonehead athletes who contribute little to civilization other than slam dunks and touchdowns. That is the inevitable world of Troy Bolton."

Gabriella smiled, not knowing what was coming.

Taylor went to another wall, saying, "But the path of the mind, the path we are on . . . ours is the path that has brought the world *these* people - "

She pointed to photos as she called out each name. "Eleanor Roosevelt . . . Frida Kahlo . . . Sandra Day O'Connor . . . Madame Curie . . . Jane Goodall . . . Oprah Winfrey, and so many others who the world reveres."

Gabriella nodded. There was no doubt those were admirable people. "But . . . what has this . . . I've got Kelsi waiting for me to rehearse. . . ."

"Gabriella, Troy Bolton represents one side of evolution . . . lunkhead basketball man," Taylor explained patiently. "And our side, the side of education and accomplishment, is the future of civilization. That's the side where you belong."

In the locker room, Troy was doing his best to defend himself to his team. "If you guys don't know that I'll put one hundred and ten percent of my guts into that game, then you don't know *me*."

"Well, we just thought – " Chad began.

"I'll tell you what *I* thought," Troy said. "I thought you were my friends – win together, lose together . . . teammates."

Chad tried to explain their side of the story. "But suddenly the girl and the singing – " He was standing next to Taylor's laptop with the video-link camera.

Troy sighed, tired of discussing this and tired of defending himself. "I'm for the team, I've always been for the team. She's just someone I met. . . ."

Troy didn't know it, but the laptop camera was transmitting the live feed of everything he was saying to the chemistry lab . . .

. . . where Gabriella, Taylor, and the rest of the Scholastic Club watched what Troy was saying.

". . . The singing thing is nothing, probably just a way to keep my nerves down, it doesn't mean anything to me," Troy was saying. "You're my guys and this is our team . . . Gabriella's not important. I'll forget the audition, forget her, and we'll go get that championship. Everyone happy now?"

Taylor froze the image on the screen. "Behold," she said. "Lunkhead basketball man. So, Gabriella . . . we'd love to have you for the Scholastic Decathlon."

Gabriella stared at the screen, crushed by what Troy said. They had shared so much - surely it had meant *something* to him?

The other girls awkwardly shuffled towards the door. No one looked at Gabriella. On her way out, Taylor said, "Do you want to grab some lunch?"

Gabriella shook her head. She just wanted to be alone.

Taylor nodded and left.

Just then, Gabriella heard noise from the quad below. She went to the window and looked out in time to see an impromptu pep rally. The basketball team was swarming around Troy, trying to pump him up for the big game.

Gabriella felt so sad, so alone. And, just as she had been doing since New Year's Eve, she started to express herself in song:

> "It's funny when you find yourself
> Looking from the outside
> I'm standing here
> But all I want is to be over there
> Why did I let myself believe
> Miracles could happen
> 'Cause now I have to pretend
> That I don't really care"

She left the chemistry lab. The halls of East High were filled with trophy cases, banners, and murals. All she wanted was to get away from Wildcat spirit, and it was impossible.

She finally got to her locker. As she began putting books into it, Troy came up to her. He was beaming, filled with energy and high spirits from the pep rally.

"Hey, how ya doin'?" he called.

She didn't look at him.

"Listen, there's something I need to talk to you about, okay?" he went on.

"And here it is," she interrupted him. "I know what it's like to carry the load with friends. I get it. You've got your boys, Troy. It's okay. So we're good."

"Good about what?" he asked, puzzled. "I need to talk to you about the final callbacks."

She tried to smile. It was better if she ended this now, rather than let him do it. She could act like it was all her own idea. At least, she thought, I'll still have my pride. . . .

"I don't want to do the callbacks, either," she said quickly. "Who were we kidding? You've got your team, and now I've got my team. I'll do the Scholastic Decathlon, you win your championship. It's where we belong." She smiled bravely. "Go, Wildcats."

Now Troy was the one who was bewildered and hurt. "But I don't - "

Gabriella didn't let him finish. "Me either," she said firmly.

She pulled the sheet music from her locker, handed it to him, and walked away.

"Gabriella!" Troy called.

She didn't respond. The bell rang, signalling the start of the next class.

Troy stared after her, stunned and hurt.

CHAPTER SEVEN

Over the next few days, Gabriella and Troy became more and more depressed. Gabriella thought Troy had dumped her. Troy thought Gabriella had dumped him. And, even though their friends tried to cheer them up, nothing worked.

One day, during PE class, Chad, Jason, Zeke, and some other students were goofing around on the outside basketball court. They were passing a ball in a circle, fast and slick, just like the

Harlem Globetrotters. Laughing, they waved at Troy, inviting him to join them.

But Troy ignored them and headed over to the track for a jog instead, moving steadily away from his friends.

That evening, Troy shot baskets alone in his backyard. He missed a few baskets and slammed the ball down in frustration. His father watched from an upstairs window, worried. He knew something was wrong. He also knew it wasn't the right time to try to find out what it was.

At the Montez house, Gabriella was sitting by her bedroom window. She was surrounded by her books, but she wasn't reading. Instead, she was gazing out the window at the stars and trying not to cry.

Her mother opened the door, holding a portable phone. She held it out to Gabriella, indicating that the call was for her.

Gabriella just shook her head.

The next day, Gabriella and Troy happened to pass each other in the cafeteria. They glanced at each other, then away . . . then defused the awkward moment by moving on without saying a word.

Chad and Taylor saw the exchange from opposite ends of the room. They looked at each other and nodded. They'd seen enough. They could see the effect of what they'd done, and they knew that they'd screwed up, big-time.

Now they had to try to fix it. . . .

Troy was sitting by himself in the rooftop garden, glumly eating a sandwich. The door opened and Chad, Zeke, and Jason appeared.

"We just had another team meeting, Troy," Chad said.

"Wonderful," Troy answered. He tried to keep the bitterness out of his voice.

Chad swallowed hard. "We had a meeting

about how we haven't been acting like a team. Us, not you. The singing thing - "

"I don't want to talk about it," Troy said shortly.

"We just want you to know that we're going to be there cheering for you," Chad finished.

Troy looked up, surprised. "Huh?"

Zeke nodded furiously. "Yeah, Cap, if singing is something you want to do, we should be boosting you up, not tearing you down."

"Win or lose, we're teammates," Chad added. "That's what we're about. Even if you turn out to be the worst singer in the world - "

" - which we don't know, because we haven't actually heard you sing," Jason pointed out.

Troy sighed. It was great to finally have the support of his buddies, but it didn't mean anything anymore. "And you're not gonna hear me sing, dudes, because Gabriella won't even to talk to me, and I don't know why."

Chad and the boys exchanged uneasy glances. "We do," Chad finally said.

Zeke pulled a bag of cookies from his backpack and offered them to Troy. "Baked these fresh today. Want to try one before we tell you the rest?"

Inside the chemistry lab, Gabriella was surrounded by Taylor and the Scholastic Club.

"We're worse than jerks," Taylor was saying earnestly, "because we're mean jerks. We thought Troy Bolton and the singing thing was killing our chances to have you on our Scholastic Decathlon team."

"Why talk about it?" Gabriella said curtly. "I heard what he had to say. I'm on your team now. Done."

"No," Taylor sighed. "Not done." She hesitated, then admitted, "Chad knew he could get Troy to say things that would make you want to forget about the callbacks. We planned it. And we're embarrassed and sorry."

Gabriella absorbed the shock of that, but she said, "No one forced Troy to say anything." She took a deep breath and went on bravely. "And you know what? It's okay. We should be preparing for the decathlon now. So it's time to move on."

Taylor shook her head. She couldn't let this defeatist attitude go unchallenged. "No, it's not," she said in ringing tones. "The Scholastic Decathlon is . . . whatever. How you feel about us, and Troy, that's something else."

That evening, Mrs. Montez opened the front door to find Troy Bolton standing on her doorstep.

"Mrs. Montez, I'm Troy Bolton," he said politely.

Her eyes widened a little. So this was the Troy she had heard about from Gabriella! She smiled. "Oh . . . Troy . . ."

She glanced over her shoulder. Gabriella was standing on the stairs, just out of Troy's line of sight. She shook her head adamantly.

Mrs. Montez raised one eyebrow, but she got

the message. She turned back to Troy and said, "Well, Gabriella is a little busy with homework and such, so now's not really a good time. . . ."

"I made a mistake, Mrs. Montez, and I need to let Gabriella know that," he said in a rush. "Could you tell her that I came by to see her?"

She nodded and smiled as she closed the door. Troy Bolton, she thought. He certainly seems like a nice boy. . . .

As Troy left, he crossed the lawn and glanced up. He saw a light go on at the far end of the second story. There was a small balcony outside the window. Suddenly inspired, Troy took out his mobile and dialled Gabriella's number.

In her room, Gabriella saw Troy's photo come up on her mobile screen. After a long moment, she answered.

As soon as he heard her voice, Troy said in a rush, "What you heard the other day . . . none of that is true. I was sick of my friends riding me about singing with you, and I said things I knew would shut them up. I didn't mean any of it."

110

"You sounded pretty convincing to me," she said coolly.

Troy looked up. He could see Gabriella walking around in her room. He looked up at the balcony for a moment, then he looked at a nearby tree. Then he started climbing.

As he climbed, he continued to talk into the phone. "The guy you met on vacation is way more me than the guy who said those stupid things."

"Troy, the whole singing thing is making the school whack," Gabriella sighed. "You said it yourself, everyone is treating you different because of it."

Troy grabbed a branch and pulled himself a few feet higher. "Maybe that's because I don't want only to be the basketball guy anymore," he argued. "They can't handle it. That's not my problem, it's theirs."

He pulled himself up onto the balcony. Gabriella was only a few feet away, but her back was to him. She didn't know he was there.

She said, "But your dad – "

"This isn't about my dad," he said, still talking into the phone. "This is about how I feel. And I'm not letting the team down. . . . They let me down. I'm going to sing. What about you?"

"I don't know, Troy."

"You need to say yes," he said. "Because I brought something for you."

Gabriella looked confused. "What do you mean?"

Troy lowered his phone and began to sing to her, directly, sweetly, honestly.

"Start of something new
It feels so right
To be here with you . . . oh
And now . . . lookin' in your eyes
I feel in my heart
The start of something new"

Gabriella turned around to see Troy standing on the balcony outside her room.

"It's a *pairs* audition," he reminded her. Then he handed her the sheet music she had given back to him. After a long shared look, Gabriella began to smile.

The next few days were a whirlwind of activity for both of them. Troy led basketball practices with energy and authority, back on top of his game. Gabriella ran through formulas with the Scholastic Club, more focused and impressive than they had ever seen her. Then they would run out of their separate practices, meet in the hall, and dash for the rehearsal room to rehearse with Kelsi.

One day, Sharpay and Ryan came out of their own rehearsal and heard Gabriella and Troy singing.

"Wow, they sound good," Ryan said.

Sharpay turned on him. "We have to do something. Our callback is on Thursday, the basketball game and Scholastic Decathlon are on Friday." She stopped. An idea - a good idea, possibly a great idea – was forming. "Too bad all of these events aren't happening on the same day at the same time."

"Well, that wouldn't work," Ryan said with his usual naïveté, "because then Troy and Gabriella couldn't make the callback."

Sharpay gave him a look and waited for the implications to sink into her brother's dim brain.

Finally, his face lit up and he said, "I'm proud to call you my sister."

Later, Sharpay and Ryan cornered Ms. Darbus and spent some minutes talking earnestly to her.

Finally, Ms. Darbus said, "So if you're telling me, as copresidents of the Drama Club, that changing the callbacks is what's best for our theatre program . . . I might actually agree with you."

She walked away. Ryan scratched his head.

"Was that a yes?" he asked his sister.

She gave him a wink that said, "Mission accomplished."

What they didn't notice - because they never noticed Kelsi - was that the shy young composer was standing nearby and had witnessed the entire thing.

Including the wink.

The next morning, Troy and Gabriella got to school early so they could meet Kelsi and work in a little more rehearsal. They found her standing in front of the bulletin board, her face ashen.

The sign on the board said: MUSICAL AUDITIONS RESCHEDULED TO FRIDAY 3:30 P.M.

Troy and Gabriella stared glumly at those fatal words.

"Same time as the game - " Troy said.

"And the Scholastic Decathlon - " Gabriella added.

Chad and Taylor - accompanied, as always, by the basketball team and the Scholastic Club - gathered behind Troy and Gabriella.

115

"Well, I just don't know why they would do that," Taylor said, honestly puzzled.

"I smell a rat named Darbus," Chad said darkly.

"Actually, I think it's two rats, neither of them named Darbus," Kelsi said.

Everyone turned to see who had spoken. It took a minute - the petite Kelsi was almost lost among all the basketball players who towered over her.

"Do you know something about this, small person?" Chad asked.

Kelsi nodded. "Ms. Darbus might think she's protecting the show, but Ryan and Sharpay are pretty much only concerned with protecting themselves."

Chad's face tightened with anger. "Do you know what I'm going to do to those two over-moussed show dogs - "

"Nothing," Troy said quickly, taking command. "We're not going to do anything to them." He grinned. "Except sing, maybe."

Troy looked at each member of the basketball team and Scholastic Club. "This is only going to happen if we all work together," he said. "Who's in?"

The teams eyeballed each other. Then Chad held up a hand. Taylor high-fived it. Everyone broke out into grins.

They were in.

On the day of the callback auditions, basketball championship game, and Scholastic Decathlon showdown, emotions were running high.

To demonstrate their newfound sense of solidarity, Chad and the basketball boys presented Taylor with a cake that Zeke had baked. The icing read: "Scholastic Decathlon Today - Support Brain Fame!"

In return, Taylor and her girls handed Chad a banner that read: "Go Wildcat Hoopsters!"

Ms. Darbus watched them sardonically. How lovely, she thought. The basketball boys and the brainiac girls are making nice. . . .

Then Chad and the boys walked up to Sharpay and Ryan and zipped open their jackets. Each one had a letter on his T-shirt, spelling out the message: "Go, Drama Club!"

Chad gave Sharpay a huge smile.

Ms. Darbus looked around at the banner, the cake, the boys with letter T-shirts, and smiled in spite of herself.

"Well, it seems we Wildcats are in for an interesting afternoon," she said drily. But her eyes were twinkling.

CHAPTER EIGHT

At three o'clock, the halls of East High were empty. Quiet filled the school. There was a sense of anticipation –

– and then the bell rang!

Doors burst open and students rushed into the halls. The school was buzzing with excitement!

In the gym, the stands were full of spectators, cheering and clapping. The school band was playing, the cheerleaders were dancing up a storm, banners were waving in the air. . . . It was time to decide who were the champions, once and for all!

In the locker room, Troy sat alone on a bench. The rest of the team had run onto the court. He could hear the crowd being whipped into a frenzy.

All those hours of practice, all those drills, all that training . . . it all came down to this night.

His dad came into the room. "How're you feeling?"

"Nervous." Troy had to be honest.

"Me, too." His dad smiled. "Wish I could suit up and play alongside you today."

Troy grinned slightly. "Hey, you had your turn."

His father looked at him seriously. "Do you know what I want from you today?"

Troy nodded. His dad didn't have to tell him. "A championship."

His dad looked Troy straight in the eyes. "That'll happen or it won't," he said gently.

"What *I* want is for you to have fun. I know about all the pressure, and probably too much of it has come from me. All I really want is to watch my son having the time of his life, playing a game we both love. Give me that, and I'll sleep with a smile tonight, no matter how the score comes out."

Troy looked at his father. A strange feeling of relief spread through him. "Thanks, coa - " He corrected himself. " - Dad."

His father smiled at him and walked away.

Blackboards had been set up on each side of the choir room - the first round of the Scholastic Decathlon was about to begin. The walls were lined with tables where contestants could conduct experiments. A few dozen chairs had been set out for judges and spectators.

As the clock ticked down, each team gathered for a final briefing.

In the theatre, Kelsi played random tunes on the piano as a few spectators wandered into the large auditorium. Ryan and Sharpay did bizarre actor-prep exercises backstage: opening their mouths wide, uttering weird vocalizations, and falling back into each other's arms to demonstrate their absolute trust in each other.

In the choir room, the decathlon teams, all wearing lab coats, faced off for the opening bell.

Gabriella stood at a blackboard, poised to begin. The moderator signalled "go," and she and the star of the competing team began scribbling formulas as fast as they could.

In the theatre, Ms. Darbus was making yet another speech. "Casting the leads of a show is both a challenge and a responsibility, a joy and a burden," she said. "I commend you, and all young artists who hold out for the moon, the sun, and the stars - "

The five kids sitting in the auditorium just stared at her. They didn't have a clue about what she meant.

Ms. Darbus sighed, and tried to end on a grand note. "So . . . shall we soar together?" She checked her clipboard, just for form's sake, and called out, "Ryan and Sharpay?"

The brother-and-sister team made a grand entrance as their recorded music started. From the very first note, it was clear that this was a two-person musical, with light cues and choreography and moves that would put most Broadway dancers to shame.

As they started singing the chorus, Sharpay and Ryan moved into all-out choreography, with kicks, spins, turns, and leaps.

Meanwhile, in the gym, the two teams who would be battling for the championship finally faced each other in centre court. This was it - all the training, all the practice drills, all the pep talks led up to this . . . very . . . moment. . . .

The ref threw the ball for the opening tip-off, and the game began! From the very first seconds, the crowd was going crazy.

Even in the choir room, the Scholastic Decathlon team could hear the crowd noise. Everyone except Gabriella, that is. She was standing at the board, totally focused on what she had to do. As the timer ticked down, she and her opponent wrote formulas as quickly as possible.

Just one last number and - she finished seconds ahead of her opponent and slammed the timer button, stopping the clock.

The moderator quickly checked her answer, then nodded. Points to the Wildcat Scholastic team! As everyone cheered Gabriella, whose face was flushed with victory, Taylor peeked at the clock. It was 3:35 P.M.

She quietly moved over to her laptop and punched in a code, murmuring to herself, "All right, Wildcats, time for an orderly exit from the gym. . . ."

Immediately, the words "message transmitted" appeared on the screen. In the gym's utility room, a small wireless router had been patched into the electronic grid. Within seconds, the router started blinking . . . the mission had begun!

Suddenly, the electronic scoreboard blinked and random numbers began appearing where the score had been. The message board began flashing. The gym lights pulsed on and off.

The players stopped in midgame, baffled as to what was going on.

Principal Matsui didn't know what was happening either, but he did know school policy. He quickly took the microphone and said, "Well, we seem to have a little electronic gremlin here. I'm sure we'll figure this out. In the meantime, per safety regulations, we all need to make an orderly exit from the gym – "

As the gym slowly emptied, Chad grinned a private grin. Phase one of the mission had been executed!

Back in the choir room, Taylor quickly hit another key on her laptop. A beaker of blue liquid was sitting on a nearby hot plate, waiting for the experiment section of the competition.

Taylor's click turned on the hot plate, which heated the liquid, which began to gurgle, which created pressure that popped off the top of the beaker - which released an awesomely bad smell in the room.

Taylor smiled in quiet satisfaction as she saw first the moderator, then the spectators, begin to react to the smell.

Within seconds, everyone had rushed out of the room.

Taylor nodded. Phase two had just been completed.

In the theatre, Sharpay and Ryan were blissfully unaware of the other dramas that were taking place in the school. They ended their song with just as much energy as when they had started. They knew they had done phenomenally well, and they took extravagant bows.

"Do you see why we love the theatre, people?" Ms. Darbus said, almost overcome with pride and joy in her star pupils. "Well done."

She made a quick check of her list and then asked, in an offhand voice, "Troy Bolton and

Gabriella Montez?" She looked around. "Troy . . . Gabriella?"

But there was no sign of them.

Kelsi looked around nervously. "They'll be here!"

Ms. Darbus shook her head with little regret. "The theatre, as I've often pointed out, waits for no one. I'm sorry."

Kelsi gave one more despairing glance at the door, but there was still no sign of her friends. She sank back onto the piano bench, crushed.

"Okay, we're done here," Ms. Darbus said briskly, drawing a line through Troy and Gabriella's names. "Congratulations to all. The cast will be posted."

Slowly, Kelsi picked up her music folder and left the stage, totally dejected.

Then Troy and Gabriella came dashing in from opposite sides of the theatre.

"Ms. Darbus! We're here!" Troy yelled.

"I called your names," Ms. Darbus said sternly. "Twice."

"Please." Gabriella couldn't believe it. After all their work, all their planning . . .

The drama teacher was firm. "Rules are rules."

But as she turned to go, she saw that something different, unexpected, in fact, altogether astounding was happening! The theatre was starting to fill with people: students and spectators from the basketball game and Scholastic Decathlon; all the members of the basketball team, led by Chad; all the members of the Scholastic Club, led by Taylor . . . they were all coming to watch the auditions!

Sharpay and Ryan watched the gathering crowd, confused. This wasn't part of their plan! Still, the theatre is all about dealing with the unexpected, so Sharpay quickly said, "We'll be happy to do our number again for our fellow students, Ms. Darbus."

The teacher shook her head, still watching with amazement as the theatre filled to capacity. "I don't know what's going on here. But, in any event, it's far too late, and we don't have a pianist."

Ryan and Sharpay smiled, relieved. Ryan looked at Troy and shrugged. "Oh, well, that's showbiz," he said happily.

Desperate, Troy said, "We'll sing without music."

Then they heard a voice - previously a timid voice, now a surprisingly bold one - call out, "Oh, no, you won't!" Kelsi charged onto the stage. "Pianist here, Ms. Darbus!"

Sharpay gave her a warning glance. "You really don't want to do that."

Kelsi set her jaw. She had had enough of taking orders from egotistical drama queens. "Oh, yes, I really do!"

She opened the piano lid with a flourish, slapped down her music, and took a seat. "Ready onstage!"

Ms. Darbus's eyes widened with delight. "Now . . . *that's* showbiz!"

Troy and Gabriella picked up their microphones and turned to face the auditorium. It was packed with people, all waiting to hear them sing.

As Gabriella looked out at all those eager

faces, she felt her face turn red. Then her knees got weak, and her stomach flipped over, and she thought she might faint.

Their first audition had been for Ms. Darbus, and they hadn't even known she was listening! Now she had to face this huge crowd.

Kelsi hit a piano key, waiting for Troy and Gabriella's nod that they were ready to begin. No one nodded. Gabriella was standing absolutely still, as if she were frozen.

Kelsi started to play, hoping that the music would help relax Gabriella and that she would start singing.

But Gabriella couldn't even open her mouth. Kelsi stopped playing and looked at Troy. What should I do?

He nodded to her to start again. And then he began to sing, directly to Gabriella.

"We're soarin', flyin'
There's not a star in heaven that we can't reach
If we're tryin', yeah, we're breaking free"

When it was Gabriella's turn, she covered her mic and said, "I can't do it, Troy. Not with all these people staring at me."

Troy glanced at the crowd. People were starting to look confused. They were murmuring to each other, "What's wrong? Is she all right?"

He turned back to Gabriella and whispered, "Look at me. Right at me. Like the first time we sang together, like kindergarten, remember?"

She did. And when she looked into Troy's eyes, he looked back the same way he did at the karaoke contest. The spark of magic flared up again, but brighter and stronger. Gabriella could feel herself relax. She could feel herself smile. . . .

Troy made a signal to Kelsi, and she started playing again. Troy sang, heartfelt:

"You know the world can see us
In a way that's different
Than who we are"

131

Gabriella smiled even wider and sang the next two lines:

"Creating space between us
'Til we're separate hearts"

Then they sang together, in perfect harmony:

"But your faith
It gives me strength, strength to believe . . ."

As they continued, their confidence - and their trust in each other - grew. They began to sing as though they were the only ones in the room.

Everyone in the auditorium was transfixed by the powerful, real emotion that Troy and Gabriella were expressing through the song.

Coach Bolton wandered into the auditorium, wondering impatiently when the electronic malfunction would be fixed and the game could resume. He looked at the stage - and he couldn't believe what he was seeing! His son was singing, in public, and - he was really, really good!

Throughout the theatre, the music was casting its spell. The brainiac girls glanced at the basketball boys, and the two groups exchanged friendly smiles. The skater dudes nodded to the drama kids - hey, if this is musical theatre, it's cool, man. All the different groups, usually so separate, were united as they watched a completely unlikely pair - Troy dressed in basketball warm-ups and Gabriella wearing a lab coat - sing to each other with genuine emotion.

As the song ended, Troy and Gabriella gazed into each other's eyes. For one long moment, there was total silence. Then Kelsi stood up and began applauding. So did Coach Bolton. Ms. Darbus called out "Bravo!" and "Brava!" over and over again. And then the entire crowd was on their feet, roaring their approval.

Even Ryan and Sharpay started applauding - then they caught themselves and quickly stopped.

Before the applause ended, Troy and Gabriella gave each other a quick hug and rushed off. After all, they had some unfinished business to attend to. . . .

CHAPTER NINE

It was the last few seconds of the championship game. The Wildcats were behind. The clock was ticking down. . . .

Then Troy suddenly flew across the court, weaving between opponents, heading for the goal. Just as he had practised, he faked right, went left, threw the ball, and . . . NOTHING BUT NET! The buzzer sounded and it was a one-point Wildcat victory!

In the melee that followed, Coach Bolton

found his son and gave him a huge hug.

Ms. Darbus fought her way through the crowd. As she approached the coach, the old adversaries eyed each other for a moment . . . then they grinned and gave each other a high five.

As Gabriella got close to Troy, he called out, "What about your team?"

"We won, too," she said, excited and happy. They hugged each other in congratulations, just as Chad handed a basketball to Troy.

"Team voted you the game ball, Captain," he said. They high-fived each other, then he turned to Taylor. "So . . . you're going with me to the after-party, right?"

"Like on a date?" Taylor asked, shocked.

"Must be your lucky day." Chad grinned.

She laughed, and nodded. A week ago, she would have disagreed, but now . . . maybe Chad was right. Maybe it *was* her lucky day.

As Gabriella walked out of the gym, still beaming, Sharpay came up to her. "Well, congratulations," Sharpay said. "I guess I'm going to be the understudy in case you can't make one of the shows, so . . . break a leg."

Gabriella looked at her, startled.

Sharpay smiled - a real smile this time - and explained, "In theatre, that means good luck."

And now Gabriella smiled a real smile, too.

As she moved on, Zeke saw his chance and moved in on Sharpay.

"Sorry you didn't get the lead, Sharpay," he said. "But you're still really, really good. I admire you so much."

"And why wouldn't you?" asked Sharpay, who hadn't changed into a completely different person, after all. "Now bye-bye."

He shyly held out a bag of cookies. "I baked these for you. . . ." She took them as if they were her due, and he walked away.

Troy found Kelsi in the crowd and handed her the basketball. "Composer, here's our game ball. You deserve it . . . playmaker."

Kelsi nearly fainted. *She* was being handed the game ball by *Troy Bolton!* She got dizzy, just thinking about how much her life had changed in one short week. Dizzy and very, very happy. She broke into a huge grin and threw the ball in the air. . . .

And when it came down, East High School was a different place. It was a place where punk kids could talk to brainiacs, and jocks could hang out with drama kids. It was a place where everybody could follow the beat of their own drummer, and other people would cheer them on. In other words, it was a place where people could have fun . . . together.

After the huge celebration ended, people were still milling around, laughing, talking, and getting to know people they had never even noticed before.

That's when Sharpay came flying into the crowd, pushing people out of the way to get to Zeke.

"Your cookies are genius!" she yelled. "The

best things I've ever tasted. Will you make some more for me, Zeke?"

Zeke grinned. *Of course* he would bake for her! In fact . . . he waggled his eyebrows and said slyly, "I might even make you a crème brûlée."